LIFE

&
DEATH

PART 2

Author- Palmwine Sounds

ISBN-(Paperback)- 978-1-917267-39-7

ISBN (E-Book)- 978-1-917267-40-3

Year Published- 2025

Published by Nubian Republic Ltd UK on behalf of Palmwine Publishing Limited Nigeria

Email: info@palmwinepublishing.com

Address-Nigeria: 1A Jos Road Bukuru, Plateau State, Nigeria.

www.palmwinepublishing www.raffiapress.com www.nuciferaanalysis.com

LIFE

& DEATH

PART 2

Palmwine Sounds

TABLE OF CONTENTS

TABLE OF
CONTENTS

TABLE OF CONTENTS

Kunta Kinte

Kunta Kinte
He hailed
From The
Gambia

The African
A fierce warrior
Strong, proud
Well-educated

Kunta Kinte
Was sailed
Far away
To slave

The African
Was flogged
Overworked
And unpaid

Kunta Kinte
Was forced
Bearing seeds
For the master

The African
Forgotten
His home
Colonised

Kunta Kinte
Wise up now
Marginalised
For too long.

Violence 2

I'm a man of peace, but test me
Without violence, there is no peace

I'm like water, have no enemies
As Fela talk, go fight, na die

Do me, I do you
Tolerance has its limit

Shege in Babylon!
Double collections!

Babylonians shall chant my name
Mournful praises give me immense joy.

No Gree

I'm stubborn, I know
I will find a way
No is another's yes

Aggressively find a way
I think my way is always best
I may be wrong — let me learn.

The Race

In this race of life
No winners or losers
We all finish in death
Can't cheat your way.

From Japa to Sapa

Not every Japa is bright
The Sapa that would flog
You long for home
Crying silent tears

You would work double-double
Like you've never worked before
Overtime becomes your friend
Longing for the night shift

Crying back home to
Friends and family
Most don't believe
Longing for comfort.

Land of the Charlies

The land of smiles
Might not be happy
But a smile is a smile
Blessed with yansh

Both male and female
Shake it with pride
Preserving their culture
In language, music, dance...

Inscribed in art, stories, folktales...
Might want to make home someday
"Akwaaba" yelled as I touch down
Eating waakye and eggs daily.

Inflation Rant

Everything don become expensive
Food, light, rent, tax, and even water

I was not forced to be born
I no come this life to suffer

Expensive opolopo (plenty)
It pains — na lie???

Miss childhood days
Ignorance was bliss

Water and food are meant to be free
It's a basic human need to survive

Mother Earth blessed us in abundance
And I'm charged to survive. What a life?

Government go even tax you
On something that is free
Most are truly born to suffer
This life no fair at all.

Uncle Innoson

A strong and steady man
No need for the publicity
Letting his works speak
His accolades endless.

Rasta Bow

String the bow of chaos, and draw
Rain wickedness onto the wicked
The righteous no fear
A righteous bow
Shall be strung
The blessing of Jah Rastafari
Resides in its righteous strings.

Trouble

You came to buy trouble from
trouble?
Best in his trade — you shall collect
Wahala his supplier — you are a joker
Organised chaos under control
Shakara and Yanga his directors
Giving him strategic advice.

Mischief

Heavy wahala strings on bass guitar
Wahala-branded drums set on stage
Giving mischief a plane to exist
Descending down like a spirit
Its form cannot be comprehended
The true master of his craft
His wife Shakara shaking tambourines
Daughters of chaos dancing to tunes
Cruise nude to such amazement
Cruise himself has been out-cruised.

No Rest

The wicked do not rest
So why shall I, a Rasta?
It cannot be possible

I shall work double
Till my goal is met
Treading over wicked

Mournful praises
Shall be my reward
Jah always guiding.

Government Magic

Government wizardry
Government bugu-bugu
Abracadabra!

Monkey don enter
One, two, three
Snake don chop

As any try to understand the magic
A spell of confusion will be triggered
The juju is very strong
Naija is not your mate.

The Mystic Men

Science is magic
Magic is science

Magic is science that can't be explained
Juju has not been over-studied

Scientists are mystic men of their craft
The elements of the universe in their control

The true avatars of the universe
Bending the periodic table to will.

Peace Treaty

The Babylonians may call for a peace treaty
No treaty will be signed, no peace offering

Or better still, sign, collect the peace offering
Backstab them — a well-deserved response

Raining chaos, lightning, and wickedness
The Rasta men shall give them no peace

Rasta knows Babylonian ways are different
Calling for peace to fabricate new
ammunition.

O Rice oh Compatriots

In rice we trust
Riot, O rice
Inflation, O rice
Palliative, O rice
Election, O rice
SARS, O rice
Protest, O rice
Hunger, O rice
Unemployment, O rice
Poverty alleviation, O rice
Insecurity, O rice
Bad governance, O rice
Bending rice like Declan Rice
Does rice solve the problem?

Hard Work

There are blessings in hard work
Might not be monetary value
Might not show immediately
Might not show in your life
Investing for future generations
In death, you look down and smile
Your seeds have finally matured
Just smile with the pains of now
Because the future shall be bright.

Perfect Imperfections

Show your imperfections
They're very perfect to me

Remove your face mask
Throw down your insecurities

I want to see your soul
Don't hide behind defenses

Put it up for the public to see
The raw you is perfect for me.

Money Magic

Money has its own jùjú
Money has its own magic
Money has its own power
Money has its own sorcery

Money is a strong enchantment
Abracadabra, the door has opened
Revolutionist has 'unrevolutionized'
The aroma may even lift pants.

Pity

I do not want your pity
I did what I did, no shame

Would I do it again?
Maybe, differently

I make no mistakes
Just a new lesson.

Koboko of Truth

I'm a soldier of Jah
My koboko of truth

Hanging from my waistline
If held in my right or left hand

Babylonians shall be lashed
Until truth is regurgitated.

Tolerance 2

I'm a very tolerant person
But tolerance has its limits

Try me once, twice, thrice
The fourth time, OYO (on your own)

I shall rain wicked chaos upon you
Zion might even beg me for your mercy.

Koboko

There are different kinds of Koboko
The one used to flog a person

Men of culture know of a dangerous form
We use trousers to cover it, tie it with a belt

That Poi stick is very dangerous
That Poi stick can give women a belly.

Fire on Babylon

Babila za ta ƙone (Babylon shall burn)
Babila za su ci wuta (Babylon would eat fire)
Zai kama wuta (It would catch fire)
Zai mu ba su wuta (We would give them fire)
Hankali, hankali (Patience, patience)
Mu Rasta ce haka (We Rasta say so).

Hail Him

His Majesty
Our Emperor
A true Rasta
Gave Rastas a home in Africa
Pan-African ideology in DNA
One that must be respected.

Rasta 🌴😡🫦 Babylon

No understanding needed
No need to comprehend it
Just serve them wickedness
Babylon should not be studied
Just look down upon them, and
Rain down wicked wickedness.

Weary

I shall not be weary
With Jah at the wheel
Bumpy roads are temporal

I shall not be weary
Anything Babylon throws
I shall stand my ground

I shall not be weary
Babylon would burn
Jah's children know this

I shall not be weary
The current journey
Is very temporal

I shall not be weary
Because tomorrow
Shall be better.

The Star
On June 14, 2002
The 'stars, ayra' aligned
A celestial being was born
God was mesmerized
By his own creation
God proclaimed
"I too dey create."

The Road to Zion

The road is a dry and heavy road
But it is the only righteous road
Politicians can't 'politicate' their way
On this road, funds are worthless

We must tread over a wicked kingdom
Babylonians would collect on the road
We still must catch cruise on the road
But for Jah's warm embrace, it's worth it.

Heart of a Child

At Zion's gate, your heart must be weighed
It shall be weighed against the heart of a child

For those who fail the test
March back to Babylon
Where you came from

Or else

Blood
Lightning and
Thunder

Shall kiss you

Outward appearances shall matter not
Only what lies within shall matter.

Test Me

I am a madman

Wicked, keep away from me

Babylon, don't cross my sight
Madness does not show on the face
Unfiltered madness acts sane
Because when it's unleashed
Chaos shall have a great feast.

Matching Fire

Get a hint of Babylon's activities
Rain down heavy wickedness
No need for investigation
No need for explanation
Then finish them up,
With the koboko of truth.

Jah's Love

Jah's love is for all
A warm blanket
Around the universe

His love is equal to all
The good, bad, and ugly
No segregation from Him.

Ashawo Tales

Ashawo go dey pursue Deborah
While still chasing Amanda
Shooting his shot at Ruth
Scoping Sophia on the side
And rizzing Halima all at once,
Playing a dangerous game.

Kudi Najeriya Na Mu
(Nigerian Money Is Ours)

Bani nawa, bari in ci
(Give me mine, let me eat)

Akwai shi da yalwa (There is plenty of it)
Kudi noma (Agricultural money)
Kudi mai da iskar (Oil and gas money)
Kudi duwatsu masu daraja
(Precious stone money)

Kudi fasaha da sana'a
(Creative and craft money)
Raba shi daidai (Divide it fairly)
Bari in samu nawa
(Let me collect my share).

Why Worry?

Don't worry yourself
Why downpress?

Problems plenty,
Focus on the now.
What can I do today?

Let tomorrow
Worry about itself.

Laziness

Laziness should not be tolerated.
Laziness is Babylonian behaviour,
Sucking Jah children like vampires,
Eating fruits they did not labour for.

It is the habit of the wicked,
Profiting off the toil of the righteous.
Lazy ones do not deserve respect.

Laziness is a contagious disease,
If not rooted out, it spreads fast.
Serve them a dish of wickedness.
The lazy shall never smell Zion's gates.
Let them forget their slice of Zion.

Wisdom

Jah, I cry and plead with thee,
Wisdom that surpasses Solomon's
Is my deepest wish and desire.
But knowing what is best,
A fraction of his will do.
I would know no wiser.

Zion

At Jerusalem...

The hill of Zion is where you want to be.
The few truths of creation reside there,
Where the prophets of Jah once dwelled.

Peaceful deliberation thrives on that hill,
And wisdom flows like a river.
Differing ideologies unite under Jehovah.

Songs of Jah echo above the hills,
Our Father, catching cruise at the top,
The proud mystery man.

Praise Jah

You must praise Jehovah.
We are part of His creation,
And that alone deserves gratitude.
Being a part of His work,
That's all we need to know.

Prayer

The only appointment you'll ever need:
Hands clapped together,
Knees on the floor,
Cry your troubles or give thanks.

He listens.
No appointments.
No bias.
No rejection.
Jah hears all.

Hustler Stories

Wake up!
Body pains for breakfast.
A shower and hot coffee ease the ache.

For lunch,
Catch up on missed sleep.
Rest fuels the weary bones.

Dinner,
Comes like a storm.
La-la land, rolling in sheets.

Moaning

There shall be weeping and moaning in
Babylon,
When fire, brimstone, and thunder descend.

When the trumpet sounds,
Chaos will rule.

The wrath of Jah
Hits different.

Babylon will stagger
As wickedness rains down.

King Solomon

The first man of culture,
Our Great Uncle Solomon.

Wisdom opolopo (plenty).
Women stood no chance.

They flocked to him like birds.
His wisdom, too mesmerising.

Even I am seduced.
I repeat,
They stood no chance.

Spread the Gospel

Go into the world and multiply,
Some of us took that too seriously.
Men of culture, I'm talking to us.

Spread the ashawo gospel.
Abraham's line must continue.

Spread It

Men of culture—
get your minds out the gutter!
I speak of the Rasta ideology.
The deaf must hear,
The mute shall speak,
The blind will see.
It is written—
In Torah, Bible, Quran.
In music—Bob, Culture, Dube...
We shall chant until all have heard.

Spread Am

Men of culture,
We have arrived.
The flower of creation blooms.
The sting penetrates.
We spread our seeds.

Call and Response

Michigan calls, Smiley smiles.
Fela's keys cry through brass.
Culture speaks through instruments.
Joseph, favourite son, responds.
Soundmakers whine, guitar strings sing.
Osita must transcribe the notes.
The music calls,
The body must respond.

The Fall

Babylon will fight hard,
But Babylon will fall harder.

Let them come.
Just look and laugh.

Babylon's ways are strange,
Don't bother trying to understand.

Right

If you are right,
You are right.

Stand your ground.
Do not be intimidated.

Because truth—
Will be revealed.

Lost Love

Looking for my lost love.
Bleeding from past pain.

Wanting to be loved for me again.
Looked in Grace—disappointed.

Looked in Tobi—insulted.
Now just craving peace.

The heart will heal,
But past scars remain.
Over time, scars fade.

Don't Stress Me

I'm not a judge,
Jehovah is the only one.

To each their own.
I no send your papa.

Dey your dey,
I dey my dey.

Don't stress me—
I won't stress you.

Rasta Music

Music of the conscious.
Music of the enlightened.

Music of the spiritual.
Music of the playful.

Music of peace and love.
Music of unity and oneness.

Music of truth and rights.
Music of social justice.

Music of freedom fighters.
Music of Jehovah.

Advice for Nigeria

Country of original suffer-heads.
Nothing works—light, water, road...
We can go on and on.
Hard work no dey pay—at all.
We protest—they kill.
So, we sit at home.
A more peaceful protest.
Nothing works—
So why should we?

Love = Mumu

To love is to be a fool.
Smiling for no reason.
Mumu button pushed.
Tough man melts.

Independent lady,
"Unindependent."
Love dey scatter dreadlocks.
It's sweet die,
I tell no lies.

My Enemies

God, harden the hearts of my enemies,
Greater joy when they fall.

Let them fight harder.
I'll just look and laugh.

Like Israelites vs. Pharaoh,
Jah never disappoints.

Rebel Reincarnate

From the line of Nazrul,
A rebel reincarnated.
Like the Avatar,
The spirit never dies.
**CAUSING ORGANISED CHAOS
ON JAH-JAH'S UNIVERSE.**
The wicked shall fear.
Babylon shall weep.

71

Dog or Cat

Are you a dog or a cat?
Do you follow,
Or carve your own path?
Are you a "yes master"?
Or master of yourself?
Are you waiting to be given,
Or can you fend for yourself?

Music and Me

My heart chants Nyabinghi.
From birth, music defined me.
Clap on the butt—lyrics commence.
My veins became bass strings.
From the heart, it flows.
Body moves to the rhythm.
Goosebumps rise,
And the body responds.
This joy—
Cannot be contained.

Ethiopia Land

Nigeria is my place of birth,
But the land of the Emperor
Holds a sacred space in me.

Set foot in Addis Ababa,
Show respect to the land.
Catch cruise in Shashamane.

Burn herbs, share thoughts
With like minds.
As we chant to Nyabinghi.

www.ingramcontent.com/pod-product-compliance
Lightning Source LLC
Chambersburg PA
CBHW070535040726

47501CB00021B/2309